FIFE COUNCIL LIBRARIES
FC683365

Lorna Doone

By R. D. Blackmore

A new version of the
favorite classic by Archie Oliver

Lorna Doone
First published in 2003 by
Hinkler Books Pty Ltd
17–23 Redwood Drive
Dingley VIC 3172 Australia
www.hinklerbooks.com

ISBN 1 8651 5581 0

Editor: Leone Peguero
Cover Illustration: Terry Riley
Illustrations: Jan Scherpenhuizen
Typesetting: Midland Typesetters
Printed & bound in Australia

The Author
R. D. Blackmore

Richard Doddridge Blackmore (1825–1900), the son of a curate, was born in England at Longworth, Berkshire. He wrote 14 novels, but none as successful as *Lorna Doone*. It has been popular among readers of all ages for more than 130 years.

Blackmore spent part of his childhood among the spectacular hills and valleys of Exmoor, in England's West Country. That's when he first heard the stories of outlaws and highwaymen, tales of adventure and romance. They formed the basis of his best-loved book.

Today, hundreds of thousands of tourists from all over the world still come to Exmoor in search of the legend of Lorna Doone.

Blackmore's home in later years was Teddington, in London. Teddington street names such as Doone Close and Blackmore Street are a reminder of where the author lived and wrote the wonderful story of a mysterious and beautiful girl called Lorna Doone.

Contents

Prologue
Exmoor, November 26, 1673

As night fell that Saturday, seven farmers were riding home from Porlock Market on Exmoor.

The moor was one of the wildest and loneliest places in all England. Any man would be afraid to be there at night, especially if the Doones were abroad and looking for bloody mischief.

A lone horseman appeared by the side of the track. The farmers knew this man by the weapons he carried and his broad shoulders clear against the sky. He belonged to the dreaded Doone family.

The man boldly rode down and, with his pistol aimed at their heads, demanded their money.

Six of the farmers handed over what they had. This was a large sum because they had sold some cattle at the market. Even so they would rather lose it all than suffer a deadly blow from a pistol.

The seventh farmer, a giant of a man sitting on his horse a little further away, waited until the Doone man came to him. "You too! Your money! I'll have it all, if you please," shouted the robber.

Riding home from Porlock market

Prologue

The farmer pretended to search in his coat pocket for money and then, without warning, gave the man a skull-cracking blow with his thick wooden staff.

Taken by surprise

The robber was taken completely by surprise. Unconscious, he tumbled from his horse and hit the ground with a dreadful thud.

A moment later, a dozen other members of the Doone family appeared from behind a haystack, some on horseback, others on foot.

Even the sight of this gang of dangerous and violent thieves didn't scare the farmer.

He galloped straight at them, hitting out with his staff. Three more Doones fell to the ground.

Such was the bravery of the attack that the cowardly Doones scattered and disappeared into the darkness. The farmer turned back to his friends, sure that he had frightened off the attackers for the time being.

But one of the fleeing men stopped, jumped off his horse and hid behind the haystack. He loaded his musket. This time it was the farmer who was clear against the sky.

The man aimed and squeezed the trigger. There was a flash as the gunpowder exploded. The musket ball flew out of the barrel with deadly speed towards its target.

Prologue

The robber aimed his musket

Chapter 1
A Hanging

My name is John Ridd and I will tell you more of this terrible murder on the moors.

Three days after that sad day it was my twelfth birthday and Master Fry, our faithful family servant, arrived at my boarding school at Tiverton in Devon. He was riding my father's horse and leading my pony behind him.

I was very surprised to see him. "You've made a long journey for nothing," I said, "it's still two weeks until the holidays."

Leaning forward in his saddle and carefully avoiding my eye, he said that it had been decided I should come home early.

"And father, how is he?" I asked, anxiously.

"He'll be at the crooked post by the farm, ready to meet you. He was too busy to come."

I was sure Master Fry was lying to me. My father always came to collect me from school!

We set out and reached the town of Dulver-ton, on the southern edge of Exmoor, the next

Master Fry arrives

day. We stopped at an inn to rest and eat. "Some hot mutton pasties for two weary men," Master Fry called out.

The smell of them was good enough to make a man give thanks for an empty stomach.

I have another memory of that day, one that would haunt me later in life. I went out into the yard behind the inn, to make sure our horses had been fed and watered.

There, I met a lady's maid. We started talking. She had a strong foreign accent. She said she was a maid to a wealthy countess and that their coach had broken down. Then she asked me the way to Watchet town.

It was the same road we would be taking.

That afternoon, we rode up the hill out of Dulverton and saw a coach and six horses pulling hard in the mud. Our horses had no trouble getting up the hill and we were soon alongside.

I looked inside the coach and saw the lady's maid I had met at the inn. Sitting beside her was a very pretty, dark-haired girl, aged about five or so. Opposite her sat an aristocratic-looking woman, and beside her, a boy, two or three years old.

The little boy waved and the woman looked

out and saw me. I raised my cap to her and she blew me a kiss. And then we were gone, galloping up the hill.

By late afternoon, a thick fog had fallen over the moor. Darkness was coming and we relied on our horses' eyes to find the way. I could just about see Master Fry in front of me, and he had fallen asleep on his horse's neck.

"Mercy," he shouted suddenly, as his horse slipped on a rock and he woke with a jolt. "Where are we?"

"I can see nothing familiar at all," I said.

"Just listen then," he replied.

We drew up our horses and listened with our hands cupped to our ears. At first there was nothing to hear, except the panting of our horses. Then came a low mournful sound of chains swinging and clanking. The hairs on the back of my neck stiffened. I knew what it was.

"Who's hanging in chains out here?" I asked. "Have they hanged a Doone?"

"Hang a Doone?" said Master Fry. "It would take a brave man to hang a Doone. Everyone's too scared of the Doones to do that."

"Who is it in chains then?"

"A sheep stealer. Jem Hannaford is his name. I heard they hanged him a few days ago."

Looking inside the coach

We passed by the gibbet where Jem was hanging. "Good night to you, Jem," said Master Fry. "May your creaking chains not spoil your dreams."

He then reminded me to keep my eyes and ears open because we were now on the Doones' warpath.

"Who's hanging in chains?"

Chapter 2
The Doones' Warpath

We were close to Dunkery Beacon, on the highest hill in Exmoor.

The Doones lit the beacon when they were out robbing, murdering and thieving, using it to guide themselves home at night.

"If they are about tonight," warned my traveling companion, "we may have to do a bit of creeping about on our bellies."

"The Doones will never see us in this fog," I said, hoping he would agree with me.

"Fog never stopped a Doone finding someone to rob and murder," he replied.

We rode on through the fog. The bumpy track led into a deep, steep-sided gully. I heard something and grabbed Master Fry's arm. Again, he cupped his hand to his ear and listened. The noise got louder and nearer. It was the sound of galloping horses and the jangling of stirrups.

"For God's sake," he cried, "get off your horse and hide! It's the Doones!"

My heart skipped a beat. We let our horses wander off to feed as we hid behind some bushes. The fog started to lift a little and I could see a group of riders coming.

Suddenly, what seemed like great sheets of fire roared into the skies. The extraordinary light lit both sides of the gully. It was the blazing Dunkery Beacon.

Through the bushes, I saw the riders in more detail. They were big men, tall and heavy. Their muskets were slung across their knees. Most

"It's the Doones!"

were wearing leather jerkins and long, bucket boots. They had thick iron plates attached to their chests and iron helmets on their heads.

Behind each rider, tied to their saddles, were piles of plunder. Some had carcasses of sheep or deer hanging there. I counted more than thirty men ride flying past.

Then I saw something I will never forget. The last rider had a child slung across his lap. I wondered who the child was. It could have been either a boy or girl.

How I wanted to know what would happen to this poor child! I was so angry that I leapt up and shouted at the riders.

Two of them turned around and one aimed his musket at me, but I heard the other call out, "He's just a little pixie. Save your gunpowder."

They galloped away.

"It's no thanks to you," cried Master Fry, angrily, "that my wife is not a widow now, what with you waving to the Doones to show them where we were."

"I was so angry that they had taken a child," I replied.

"That child, whoever it is, will not live long," he said grimly. "The Doones will see to that."

We went and found our horses and set off

again on the road home.

As I suspected, my father never came to meet us at the crooked post by our farm that we called Plover's Barrows.

I knew something terrible had happened. As we neared the farmhouse, I heard the sound of women crying . . .

Chapter 3
My Father's Murder

I soon learned of my father's fate. He had been killed by the Doones while riding home from Porlock Market that terrible Saturday night.

A single shot fired by a man beside the haystack had killed him. There was no reason for the shooting of my father, other than he was trying to protect the six other farmers with him; all sober and well-behaved men. My father would have nothing to do with any man who drank too much.

My mother Sarah and my two sisters, Annie and Lizzie, discovered the murder when my father's horse returned home all alone with blood on its flanks.

Father was found soon after on the moor, with his wooden staff broken beneath him.

No boy ever loved his father better than I loved mine. And no woman ever loved a husband as much as my mother did. And Annie, two years younger than I, told me how my

Killed by the Doones

mother had done a very brave thing on the Monday after his death.

She had put on her cloak and, not saying a word to anyone, set off on foot for Doone Valley. It was a place that none of us had ever visited, nor dared to. It was the home of the Doones.

She reached the entrance to the valley, a narrow rocky place known as the Doone Gate. She was met by guards with muskets and asked what business she had. She demanded to see the Doones' leader, Sir Ensor Doone.

My mother was blindfolded, taken through the Doone Gate and led down a track with a musket at her back. The guards were clearly under orders to make sure no stranger ever found out the secrets of the way into the valley. When the blindfold was removed, my mother saw an extraordinary sight.

She was standing at the head of a deep green valley. It was completely surrounded by a wall of sheer rock about a hundred feet high. At the top of that rocky cliff, wooded hills swept up almost to the sky.

In the middle of the valley, running its entire length, was the River Bagworthy. It seemed to appear from underground at one end and

Doone Valley

vanish into the rocks at the other. On either side of the river were several stone-built cottages.

Deep in this quiet valley all was peaceful. Yet this was the home of the most violent gang of robbers and murderers ever seen in England.

Chapter 4
The Doones' Story

How the Doones came to be living near us, I must explain. The Doone family was of noble ancestry as we farmers of Exmoor were all too aware.

Some thirty years earlier, they had lived in Scotland. There Sir Ensor Doone and his cousin, the Earl of Lorne, jointly owned some land. They had fought over it for many years. Then the King decided to give the land to the Earl.

Sir Ensor became so angry that he killed one of the King's servants. The King immediately banished Sir Ensor forever.

That's when the Doone family, led by Sir Ensor, came south and settled in Doone Valley. Ever since then they had plotted how to get their Scottish lands back.

Local country folk were kind to the Doones at first, bringing them presents of bacon, mutton and venison. That stopped when they saw that the Doones were too lazy to work.

At first, there was only Sir Ensor, his son Counsellor Doone, grandson Carver, a few men and some servants. They started their villainy by carrying off local farmers' daughters for their men to marry.

Soon women clutched their children in fear, and every man turned pale at the very name of a Doone. Even our local magistrates were too frightened to take action against these devils.

Revenge was swift if anyone dared to strike a Doone. One night they robbed a rich man's house. As they were leaving, someone in the household fired a shot and wounded one of them.

The gang murdered everyone and burned the house to the ground. No Doone was ever brought to trial for the crimes. Exmoor was such a remote place, many days travel from London. So it was almost lawless.

The Doones living in the valley were all huge men, tall and broad. There was a reason for this. At the age of twenty, each son or grandson was tested and measured for size and strength.

First, he had to lift 400 pounds and, then, to stand on his naked feet and touch the top of Sir Ensor's door frame with his forehead. Finally, he had to be able to fill the doorframe with his shoulders. The door was more than six feet tall and nearly three feet wide.

If the man being measured could not pass these tests, he was thrown out of the valley.

This was the place where my mother now found herself.

Chapter 5
A Mother's Anger

My mother was led to the leader's house, trembling but determined to speak her mind. She was only a common farmer's widow. What right had these men to murder her husband?

My mother took strength from her dead husband. She could feel him at her side, a strong arm around her. He seemed real enough to tell her how he liked his bacon cooked.

A tall man with long white hair met her. It was Sir Ensor Doone. He scowled at my mother and asked her what business she had with him.

"Traitors! Cutthroats! Cowards," she declared. "I have come here to find out who killed my husband."

My mother's angry outburst quite shook the man.

"Madam," said Sir Ensor, who was born a gentleman, although a very bad one, "I know nothing of this. If any wrong has been done,

"Traitors! Cutthroats! Cowards!"

you may trust a Doone to set it right."

Sir Ensor turned to one of his guards and ordered him to fetch his son, Counsellor.

"My boys are a little wild at times, I know," continued Sir Ensor, "but they wouldn't willingly harm anyone."

Counsellor came in. He was a solid man of enormous strength. He had a gray beard and thick eyebrows.

"Counsellor," said Sir Ensor, "here is a good woman."

"Only a poor woman," said Counsellor.

"She is a lady of good repute," repeated Sir Ensor, "and she says that we have killed her husband."

"Murdered him! Murdered him!" cried my mother.

"Justice shall be done," said Sir Ensor. "Tell us what you know, Counsellor."

"I will tell you, and briefly," he said, beginning his story. "Four or five of our best-behaved men went to Porlock Market on Saturday and bought some household goods. On the way home they stopped by a haystack to rest.

"The night was dark and suddenly a robber of great strength and size galloped into the middle of us. Clearly he was about to kill our men and steal our goods. He had already struck down three of the men when the last man, your brave grandson, Carver Doone, tried to fight him off.

"It was brave Carver who saved our lives, but unhappily someone's gun was accidentally fired and the farmer was hit. We had hoped it was just a flesh wound but we were all running for our lives by that time."

My mother could not believe a word. It was a pack of lies. Worse was to come.

Sir Ensor spoke to my mother. "Madam, we are gentlemen enough to forgive your husband for attacking our men. He cannot have known right from wrong. Perhaps he had drunk too much cider or beer."

On hearing these lies, my mother stormed out of the room in a fury.

Chapter 6
John goes Fishing

As time passed, my mother said how I grew more like my father every day. All the family still missed him greatly, and I wished that time would pass quickly, so that I could take my place as the man in the family.

I grew up with a great love for the country around our farm. I was always out walking across the fields and moors, exploring.

There is one day that I shall never forget. It was St. Valentine's Day in the year 1675 and I had just turned fourteen years old. My mother had been ill and wanted me to catch some fish for her.

I set out with my fishing rod. I took off my shoes, put them in a bag I had around my neck and waded into the Lynn River, the stream nearest our farm.

The water was icy cold and I didn't catch a single fish, despite wading for a mile or so. I sat down on the bank for a rest, rubbing my toes to get them warm.

Finally I decided I could not return home without any fish for mother, so I went to the very edge of Doone Valley and started fishing in the River Bagworthy.

I was a little afraid, but my father had told me a hundred times never to be a coward. And there were plenty of fish. I caught some with my rod, others I tickled beneath their undersides until they were so relaxed that I could snatch them out of the water.

My father had taught me that difficult trick. I put them all in my bag and was about to return home when I decided to explore further up the river.

I found a spot where the river raced into a great whirlpool, full of the blackest water I had ever seen. Ahead, I could hear the deep roar of more water. I walked towards the sound. It was a place I had never explored before.

There was a waterfall, the water rushing down along a rocky slide towards me. Above, I could see the waters crashing out from a dark cavern. I felt scared.

Then I said to myself, "John Ridd, these pools and awesome rocks are making a coward of you." I knew I had to explore further.

I began to climb the waterfall. It took a long

time to reach the cavern at the top. And no sooner had I dragged myself to the entrance than I slipped.

What happened next, I am not sure, but I fell into the cavern and tumbled down a rocky shaft. My body was battered and beaten as I fell. I was sure I was going to die, and no one would ever find my body in that black hole.

Suddenly, I felt a blinding pain. I found that I was caught between two large rocks. The bag holding the fish and my socks and shoes was still around my neck.

Only half conscious, I freed myself from the rocks and saw daylight. I crawled towards it. That was the last thing I remembered. Then I passed out.

John falls into the cavern

Chapter 7
First Meeting with Lorna Doone

I woke to find a young girl kneeling over me. She was gently stroking my face with a handkerchief.

"Oh, I am so happy," she said. "I thought you were dead. Now you must make sure you get better."

I had never heard such a sweet voice. Neither had I seen such a beautiful girl. She had large dark eyes, which looked down at me so gently, and her long, dark hair tumbled over her shoulders. As my head began to clear, I saw that she was sitting near some primroses.

"What are those things in your bag?" she asked.

"You had better leave them alone," I warned. "They are fish for my mother."

"Dear me," she said, laughing at the way I had been so selfish about my catch. "They are only fish. Your mother must be very poor."

First Meeting with Lorna Doone

A young girl was kneeling over John

"No," I said, a little angrily, "we are rich enough to buy this great meadow here if we wanted."

"And what is your name?" she asked, as if she was used to asking questions of lesser folk than herself.

"John Ridd. What is yours?"

"Lorna Doone," she said in a quiet voice. "My name is Lorna Doone. Surely you have heard of it."

I had never heard of a Lorna Doone, yet I knew the dreadful Doone name. I could not imagine that someone as beautiful or gentle as Lorna could be a Doone.

I offered her some of my fish. My kindness seemed to please her, but she graciously refused, saying my mother would have greater need of them.

I was only a farmer's boy and she was, no doubt, a fine lady. Her dress was bright and rich, and the material of a wonderful quality. I looked at her again. She must have been about eight years old.

"Why ever did you come here?" she asked. "Do you know what the Doone men would do if they found you here with me?"

"Beat us?"

"No. They would kill us both and bury us here."

"Why would they kill us?" I asked.

"Because you have found a secret way into Doone Valley. They would never allow you to know this and live."

Lorna begged me to go before anyone found out. "I do like you very much," she said, "and I would like to be friends. But it is not safe for us to meet."

"I will come to see you again," I answered, boldly.

Lorna suddenly looked alarmed. "Hush!" she whispered.

We had both heard someone calling her name.

Chapter 8
A Lucky Escape

Three huge men were approaching. Lorna looked so helpless and frightened!

"Come with me," I said urgently. "I'll carry you home and Mother will look after you."

"No!" she cried. "They are only looking for me. They won't harm me."

The voices got nearer. "Where has our Queen gone?" said one.

Lorna whispered to me. "They always call me their "Queen", because my fate is to marry their next leader when I grow up."

She was clinging to me, and I could feel her heart beating furiously. "They are bound to see us," she said.

I saw a way out. "I'll slip into the stream and you must pretend to be asleep."

"You must never come again," she warned me. "If they don't kill you now, they will next time."

I slipped into the water and swam to a spot

Hiding in the stream

under the bank, covering my head with weeds. I looked across the stream and saw the three men approach Lorna.

"Here's my Queen," said the largest of the three men, a real giant. "Here she be, fast asleep."

He picked up Lorna with one hand and put her on his wide shoulders, and marched away with the other men.

The valley was growing dark as the sun sunk below the hills, but I could still see Lorna. She looked back and waved as they vanished into the rising mist.

I waded out of the stream, shivering with cold, and found the rocky opening from which I had found my way into the valley.

Soon I stood inside the same rocky shaft I had fallen down. I was in a sort of secret bower. I could see where Lorna had placed wild flowers around the walls.

I heard the sound of water high above, where it roared out of the rock and down the waterfall I had climbed.

I was terrified of making that climb. My teeth were chattering with both fear and cold. But I had to. I climbed upwards, using holds in the rock to pull myself up.

I discovered that I wasn't the first person to climb this way. An old rope ladder helped at the most difficult parts of the climb. Soon I was nearing the top.

At last, I reached the ledge where the waterfall began. I slipped and slid all the way down it and hurried home.

My mother had supper on the table by the time I arrived, and everyone was ready to eat. They tried to get me to say where I had been, but I would tell no one.

In the days that followed, I thought a lot about Lorna and my adventures in Doone Valley. I had a strange feeling that, as well as having to look after my own family, I might also have to take care of Lorna Doone one day.

Chapter 9
A Famous Highwayman Arrives

The ducks quacked in alarm, as a rider came into the farmyard on a beautiful mare. He was about twenty-five years-old, short, and his legs were bowed from too much riding.

"Well, young man, what are you gaping at?" he laughed.

"Your mare," I replied. "I never saw such a beauty. Will you let me ride her?"

"Think you can ride her?" asked the man. "I doubt it."

"Give me a chance," I cried, proudly. "There's not a horse on Exmoor that I can't handle. I only ride bareback, so you can remove the saddle."

My thirteen-year-old sister Annie tried to stop me, but the man removed the saddle and said he would give me a chance.

I was quickly up on the mare's back and started her at a walking pace. She seemed very gentle.

Oh, how wrong I was! Her master gave a sharp whistle. First, the mare reared up and struck me on the nose with her neck.

Finding that I was still clinging to her, the horse sped off at a terrifying pace. She jumped the yard gate and a tall hedge, and flew across

The horse sped off

the home meadow.

Suddenly, the man whistled again. The mare stopped and quietly walked all the way back to him. I was amazed at the control he had over his horse.

I relaxed and sat up again. I must have relaxed a little too much, because I clumsily slid off the horse's back and fell in a muddy puddle. Everyone watching roared with laughter.

The man helped me up. "Well done, lad. I never thought you would stay on so long," he said.

It was then that I asked his name. "I'm Tom Faggus, as everybody knows," he said. "And this is my young mare, Winnie."

What a fool I was! I should have known it was our cousin, the famous highwayman. I had never met him before. He had come for supper with us.

The horse was as famous as its rider.

Annie cooked the meal that night and Tom praised both her food and her pretty looks. She paid him plenty of attention too.

***

Later, Tom took me out to where Winnie was stabled. She ran to him as if he was her father. Then he gave me a leather strap and asked me to pretend to whip him. Immediately, Winnie grabbed me by my belt with her teeth and lifted me clean off the ground.

"Now," said Tom, "have you ever known a horse protect its master like that? If ever I am in danger, I only have to whistle. Winnie would break down the stable door to come to my rescue."

I know all the family loved Tom Faggus, but whether we were all proud of him or ashamed I cannot judge.

A local squire, Sir Robert Bampfylde, had taken Tom to court. Sir Robert claimed that the land where our cousin grazed his cattle belonged not to Tom, but to him. Sir Robert, being wealthy and having noble friends, won the case and Tom was thrown off his land.

Tom decided that if people like Sir Robert could steal off him, then he would steal from others to survive. So he became a highwayman, and a hero among the country people.

Innkeepers kept him safe from the law, crowds drank his health, while children watched out at crossroads and alerted Tom to any law officers.

Winnie grabs John by his belt

Tom had never drawn blood or injured anyone during his robberies. He never robbed a poor man either.

Everyone cursed the Doones for their robberies, but they all liked Tom!

Chapter 10
Another Robbery

Another visitor to our farm was my mother's uncle, Reuben Huckaback.

Uncle Ben, as we called him, owned the best shop in Dulverton, and it was said that he was the richest man in town.

One year, when I was nearly twenty-one, my mother invited him to stay with us for New Year's Eve. We expected him to arrive by lunchtime, but there was no sign of him. I set out on foot to find him.

The mists were rolling in over the moor. I had walked some distance when I heard a man talking to himself nearby. It sounded as if he was praying.

"Lord," the voice was saying, "please don't leave me lost out here."

As if answering his call, I sprang from the bushes and called out, "Uncle Ben!"

He was on a horse but tied across it with heavy ropes. "I've been robbed," he cried, "by

Another Robbery

"I've been robbed."

the Doones!"

I untied him and led him safely back to the farm. We sat him down in a corner by the fire and gave him some food.

"I'm sixty-five years-old," he moaned, "and I've never been robbed before. The Doones will pay for this."

On New Year's Day, Uncle Ben and I set off to visit Baron de Whichehalse, the local magistrate. Uncle Ben wanted Sir Ensor Doone and his seven sons arrested for robbery.

"Which of the Doones attacked you?" asked the Baron.

"Sir Ensor and his seven sons."

"Are you sure it was his seven sons?" asked the Baron. "Are you even sure they were Doones?"

"Of course they were Doones!"

"You saw them in the fog?"

"I didn't have to see them," snapped Uncle Ben. "No one else would have robbed me on the moor."

"If you didn't see their faces, I can't arrest them," said the Baron.

Uncle Ben was furious. "You call this justice? The law's an old fool."

Baron de Whichehalse, who many believed

was in the pay of the Doones, waved my uncle away.

Outside, Uncle Ben turned to me. "I will take my case to the King himself, or to the Lord Chief Justice. He has the power to send men to the gallows."

That was true. The man he meant was the well-known Judge Jeffreys.

The next day Uncle Ben asked me to show him the valley where the Doones lived. So we rode up a hill on our land that gave a clear view of the valley. Uncle Ben told me he wanted to see how difficult the valley was to attack.

To me it looked impenetrable, yet Uncle Ben didn't agree.

"The Doones are fools," he said. "If we put three cannons on a nearby hill and three on top of this one, we can blast them to pieces."

I did not think an attack on the valley could be that simple, but in any case I was not listening to Uncle Ben anymore.

I was looking down at the spot where I had escaped from the Doone men seven years earlier. There I saw a figure. It was Lorna Doone.

Chapter 11
Doone Valley Again

It was Saint Valentine's Day – the very day that I had first met Lorna seven years before – when I returned to Doone Valley.

Now twenty-one years old, I was tall and strong. I had even become the local wrestling champion.

I passed the black whirlpool and found the waterfall again. It was still difficult to climb.

I reached the top, made my way down the shaft and came out at the spot where I had first met Lorna. She was there by the stream and sitting among the primroses. It was as if she had not moved in seven years.

At first, she did not recognize me. I had almost doubled in height since our first meeting. She was about to run off when I called out her name.

She knew me then, and smiled. "I remember you, how could I not?"

"Do you remember how you waved to me as

Sitting among the primroses

that great man carried you away on his back?"

Lorna said she remembered everything. Then she reminded me again of the danger in coming. "I don't think you realize what sort of people the Doones are," she said.

"I know enough of the Doones," I answered. "And I will come again to see you. I will bring you some fresh eggs from the farm."

Lorna smiled warmly, her large eyes staring into mine.

"If you must, then leave your presents in my secret bower."

Lorna's bower was just inside the entrance to the rock shaft.

I wanted to kiss her cheek, but instead she held out her hand and I kissed that.

I knew that I had fallen in love with Lorna Doone. All the following week I thought about her and wondered whether I should go to see her again.

I decided to seek the advice of Mother Melldrum, the wisest witch that ever lived on Exmoor. She lived alone in a little stone cottage, high on a lonely hillside. No man dared pass her cottage after dark. I set off on foot early in the day.

Soon the woman came in sight. Long white

The wisest witch on Exmoor

hair tumbled down her neck. Deep wrinkles covered her face. “What have you come for, John Ridd?” she asked.

I was surprised. “How do you know my name?”

“It’s no magic,” she answered. “There was a child once, who was drowning in a pond on the moor. You saved that child. You didn’t know her, but she was my granddaughter.”

I soon lost my fear of Mother Melldrum and she asked what I wanted.

“I want to know when I can next go and see Lorna Doone.”

“Is she a child of the men who killed your father?”

“I don’t know, for sure. Does it matter?”

Mother Melldrum looked at me closely. “It could matter very much to your mother. My advice is that you should have nothing to do with a Doone.”

I had never felt so sad. In the days that followed, I could not get Lorna’s face out of my mind. I even carved a heart with her initials on an old elm tree.

That’s when I decided to ignore Mother Melldrum’s advice and go to see Lorna again.

Chapter 12
Lorna Doone's Story

I found Lorna in her usual place outside the bower and gave her the two dozen eggs I had brought. Instead of thanking me she burst into tears. "Why are you crying?" I asked.

"Because you have been too kind, and I am not used to being treated kindly in this valley."

Lorna sat down beside me on a rock and I asked her to tell me about her life.

"I know little about my early life," she said. "I think Sir Ensor Doone is my grandfather. He treats me well enough, but his son Counsellor refuses to talk to me when I ask him questions about who my parents were. And Counsellor's son, Carver, I hate.

"I have no memory of my parents. But they say I am the daughter of Sir Ensor's eldest son. They say I am an heiress and call me their Queen.

"But what I want to know – and this is something no one will tell me – is why I have to live in Doone Valley, the home of men set on violence and robbery. I seem to live under a curse that will never be broken. My only happiness is Gwenny, my young maid.

"There was one other who might have been my friend. One day I was close to the bower here when a man appeared. He said I was his cousin and that he came from Scotland.

"When I told him my name was Lorna Doone, he said he knew and that he had been searching for me for a long time.

"But then a horrible thing happened. Carver discovered us together. Carver leapt at him with a sword and struck him down, swearing that no one would ever steal the Doones' Queen.

"The gentleman was no match for Carver. I couldn't watch after a while, but I heard Carver drag him off. He was never seen again. Carver Doone killed that man."

Lorna could tell me no more. She broke into helpless weeping and I held her gently in my arms. I was now more puzzled than ever. Who was she?

I returned home that night to find that we had a visitor, Marwood de Whichehalse, the son of the Baron. We had been to school

Lorna bursts into tears

together although I had never liked the silly young man. He had been riding home from a day's hunting and had called into Plover's Barrows to see Annie.

She disliked everything about him, but he was determined not to leave before he had kissed her. He caught her in the dairy. I arrived home at the same time and saw him with his arm around her. She was very upset.

Perhaps I did wrong, but I caught him a great blow with my fists and sent him flying into the milk pans. Marwood stumbled away, found his horse and rode off.

The next day a letter of apology arrived. Marwood was such a fool; the day after that he turned up again, pretending we were still the best of friends.

Annie was not interested. She only had eyes for a certain highwayman, the lively Tom Faggus.

John fights Marwood

Chapter 13
A Summons from the King

Soon after I had heard Lorna's story, another unexpected visitor arrived at Plover's Barrows.

"Listen to me, you yokel!" he roared, reining in his horse. "I am here on the King's business. Is there any place in this cursed county called Plover's Barrows?"

"You have reached Plover's Barrows, and welcome, sir," said I. "There are mutton pasties and ale for supper too."

"Now that is a welcome invitation," said the man. "I have been sitting in this saddle for ten days without the taste of a good meal. And what's more, a rogue on a strawberry mare has been following me all the way. Tom Faggus, for sure. He might have robbed me at any time if I had been worth the trouble."

I didn't blink an eyelid at the mention of Tom, but shouted to Annie to put on more pasties for our visitor.

"Now, my man," said the new arrival, "I'm looking for John Ridd."

"You have found him. I am he."

"John Ridd, in the name of the King, I give you this."

The man passed me a parchment. It was tied with a black cord and sealed in red wax. I opened it and started to read. "In the name of the King, you are ordered to appear at the Court of Westminster in London to give evidence on matters of vital interest to the safety of your King and country."

For a moment, I was terrified. Had I done something wrong? Was I to be hanged? But the man said I was not to worry. "We are not going to skin you. We just want to talk," he said. "Now let's get on with the important business . . . eating!"

The man was called Jeremy Stickles, a soldier and servant of the King. I asked him when we must leave for London. At first, he said that we should set off in the morning. But after tucking into my mother's supper that night, he suggested he might rest his horse for another day.

"I saw a turkey out in the yard," he said. "Could we not kill that for supper tomorrow?

I would enjoy some turkey."

He ate the whole bird. It was obvious that Jeremy Stickles could eat for England!

***

Now, a journey to London in those days was a most dangerous and hazardous adventure. I was unhappy to leave my mother and sisters, but Jeremy was a kind man and tried to cheer me up with jokes and stories.

He knew all about London and soon I couldn't wait to get there to see the things he described. We became the best of friends on that journey, and Jeremy even learned to forgive Tom Faggus.

For wherever we stayed the night, I let it be known that I was a relative of the famous highwayman. The result was that we were given the best rooms and the best food.

Riding to London with Jeremy

Chapter 14
The Hanging Judge

After several days' journey we reached the edge of London. Oh, what a busy place it was!

Horse-drawn coaches rushed down the lanes, footmen dashed about, courtiers strutted here and there and shopkeepers called out, trying to sell their wares.

Jeremy left me at the King's Court in Westminster, where I was summoned before the Lord Chief Justice, Judge Jeffreys. He had probably sent more men to the gallows or the executioner's block than he could remember. Thankfully, he seemed to like me.

"John Ridd," he said, "is it true to say there is a nest of robbers and outlaws living close to you?"

"Yes, my Lord," I answered.

"And why doesn't the local magistrate hang them or cut off their heads?"

"He is afraid of them. The outlaws are of high birth and their valley is hard to attack.

They will never be taken to the executioner's block."

Judge Jeffreys smiled. "We may see about that. Now tell me, how many of these rogues are there?"

"There are about forty of them, besides the women and children."

"And how long have they been there?"

"Thirty years," I replied.

Then Judge Jeffreys asked if there was a Baron de Whichehalse living near me.

"There is, my Lord."

"And is he a friend of the Doones?" he asked.

I had no real idea then whether the Baron supported the Doones and told the judge so.

He was pleased with my answer. I was quite sure from our conversation that Uncle Ben Huckaback had made a complaint to him about how the Doones had attacked him and how the Baron de Whichehalse had refused to take action against them.

Then he asked, "Do you know a man called Thomas Faggus?"

I could not lie. "He is my cousin," I replied nervously.

I was surprised when the judge said he'd heard how Tom had been robbed of his land by

The City of London

Sir Robert Bampfylde. "Tom Faggus is a good man," he said. "I know he was robbed. But I still fear he'll end up on the gallows, unless he mends his ways."

Judge Jeffreys questions John

That was almost the end of our meeting, but he had a last serious question for me. "Have you heard any talk of rebellion against the King?"

I told him that I'd heard nothing. But I did defend the other farmers who lived around Plover's Barrows. "We are good and loyal folk. We support and love our King."

"That is good," he answered. "Yet I've had reports of rebels; people who would turn the King off his throne and replace him with another."

He looked me even closer in the eye, so close that an icy shiver ran down my spine. "John," he said, "You may meet these rebels, but my advice to you is to stay clear of them!"

Our meeting ended with a final warning. "Now, John, get you gone. I shall remember you and I'm sure it will be many a day before you forget me."

No one was surer of that than I.

***

Jeremy Stickles told me later that Judge Jeffreys was considering sending some troops to attack the Doones. Soon after, I set off home alone.

My journey was safely completed thanks to Tom Faggus. He told all the innkeepers and other highwaymen on the road that I would be passing by. I was treated right royally all the way.

My family was so pleased to see me. Yet, there was another loved one I was desperate to see.

Chapter 15
Secrets of the Heart

I was keen to tell my mother about Lorna and how much I loved her. But I couldn't. The thought of my father's terrible death at the hands of the Doones was too much. I did not want to make her feel even worse about her loss.

So I hurried off by myself a few days later and climbed the hill, which I now called my "spy hill". I looked down into the valley. There, by her bower, was Lorna.

I quickly found my way into the valley and was soon with my sweetheart again. I told her all about my time in London and how I had missed her terribly.

"I thought of you every day," she replied.

She looked worried and said she had something to tell me. I guessed what she was going to say. "Do they want you to marry Carver Doone?" I asked.

"Yes, but not yet," she answered. "I am only

seventeen and he is twice my age. But they want me to promise that I will marry him when I am old enough."

She seemed so sad. I put my hand in my pocket and took out a small sapphire ring that I had bought for her in London. I held up her left hand and slipped it on her finger.

She smiled for a moment, then took the ring off and started crying. "You are so kind and loving, John," she said, "but I can't wear it yet. I dare not. Carver would see. But I will wear it one day. Keep it for now. Soon I will earn your love. And then I will be happy to wear it."

I knew then that Lorna had begun to love me a little already.

***

I hadn't told either of my sisters about Lorna. I definitely wouldn't have told young Lizzie. She and I were very different. She loved books and studying. And she never lost a chance to remind me that, as I was now head of the house, I should have taken revenge for the murder of my father.

I got along very well with Annie, although I wasn't ready to tell her about Lorna yet.

"I can't wear it yet. I dare not."

But one day she accused me of keeping secrets. I replied that it was she who was being secretive. "How about Tom Faggus?" I said. "I know you're sweet on him and he's been here several times when you were in the house alone. We all like him, but he is still a highwayman."

"And don't you have secrets, John?" she answered, angrily. "I'm sure you could hang a Doone as easily as a highwayman. Not Lorna Doone though."

I was shocked to learn that my sister knew about Lorna and I.

I guessed Lorna's maid Gwenny and our servant Betty had been talking together. That's how Annie found out.

Chapter 16
A Message from Lorna

That summer we heard gossip about people in open rebellion against the King. Some said men had been seen practicing marching and using guns on Exmoor!

The talk frightened me because I knew my mother was so kind-hearted that she would give refuge to a King's man or a rebel if they needed help.

What would Judge Jeffreys make of that? One thing I did know and that was, if I were to be hanged, my last thoughts would be of Lorna Doone.

I climbed Spy Hill daily to watch for any sign of Lorna. Strangely, she was not to be seen for several days, but I did get my first real look at Carver Doone.

I had left the hill and climbed down to Lorna's bower, and was about to creep out into the valley. Suddenly, Carver walked right past me.

John's first look at Carver Doone

He was a huge man, wearing a broad-brimmed hat, a leather jacket and breeches. His boots came up to his thighs. He was carrying a musket.

I squeezed back into the bower and held my breath. He came closer and closer. I thought my lungs would burst.

His brutal face turned my stomach. He had cruel eyes and his black beard tumbled down below his chin. Carver also had thin, mean lips.

He had no idea I was there and walked away, though not before taking the eggs that I had left for Lorna a few moments earlier.

With no sign of Lorna, I set off for home.

At supper that evening, our servant Betty winked at me and said she wanted help in the pig yard. I was puzzled, but I went out with her.

"Do you love Lorna Doone?" she whispered.

I knew then that both she and Annie knew my secret. I told her I did and she said that Gwenny had been to see her and given her a message. Lorna wanted to see me.

***

The sun was rising over Doone Valley as I climbed the water slide and reached our hideaway. Lorna was already there, looking very worried.

"They have been keeping me a prisoner in my house," she said. "Even now, I am risking my life. They suspect something. Carver found the eggs you left by the bower and wanted to know where they came from!"

I was worried about Lorna's safety. It was time for me to be bold. I told her how much I loved her. "Lorna, I love you with all of my heart. And although I am so far below you in birth and nobility, I can wait no longer. Will you promise to marry me?"

To my delight, she said she was ready to wear my ring. She put it on her finger and glanced up through her lovely eyelashes and spoke. "You have won me, John, with your bravery and kindness. I know I love you now."

We kissed. Yet even at the happiest moment of my life, she suddenly burst into tears. "Our marriage can never be!" she wept. "Something in my heart tells me that it can never happen. Carver Doone will make sure of that."

I knew then that one day Carver and I would have to meet face to face.

A meeting at sunrise

Chapter 17
The Ring

I arrived home and was met by Lizzie. "Mother is so upset," she said. "She has found out that Tom Faggus wants to marry Annie."

"That's no surprise to me," I said, trying to make the news sound unimportant. "I knew about that a long time ago."

With that, I went straight to comfort Annie. She was crying. I put my arm around her. "Don't worry," I said, "I have some news for mother that will make her think Tom Faggus would make a wonderful husband for you."

Annie was keen that I didn't mention Lorna Doone at the same time. Two shocks in a day would be too much, she said.

"No, I will tell her all today," I answered. "It will work out for the best. I know Mother. First, she will be angry with you, then with me, then with both of us. She'll remember when she was first in love with Father. Then she'll burst into tears and forgive us."

John comforts Annie

Later, I did tell Mother all about my love for Lorna and how cruel the Doones were to her.

I also explained how Judge Jeffreys, the most powerful man in the land after the King, had said he thought Tom Faggus was a good man. More importantly, I said that I was sure he would soon give Tom a pardon.

Mother's reaction was exactly as I had told Annie. And by the time the sun went down over our beautiful farm, she had already forgiven us.

***

Over the next few weeks, Lorna made it clear that I must not risk my life by crossing Carver Doone's path again. My mother was also worried and often talked of how I could bring Lorna to Plover's Barrows.

Stealing Lorna from Doone Valley was not impossible, and when I next saw her, I told her how Mother was keen for her to come to our farm.

Lorna replied very firmly that although she disliked the cruel Counsellor Doone and was terrified by Carver, she could not leave the valley until her grandfather, Sir Ensor Doone, had died. He, at least, had some love for her, she said.

She asked me how long I would wait for her. "For all my life," I said. "And how long will you wait for me?"

"Forever," she said. "The ring you gave me binds us together, forever!" Then she surprised me by taking a ring from her pocket. "I have had it in my possession since I was a child. It was part of a necklace. It is a giant's ring so it should fit you. I want you to wear it."

I took it and saw that it seemed a valuable piece. "Lorna," I said. "This is not a giant's ring. It is called a thumb-ring."

It fitted on my thumb perfectly and I asked her if she knew from where the ring and the necklace had come. All she could remember was that Sir Ensor had taken the necklace to look after, but had given her the ring to keep.

That puzzled me and I wondered if the ring or the necklace held any clues to her true identity.

Chapter 18

The Return of Jeremy Stickles

Autumn soon arrived, with the excitement of Guy Fawkes Night. As good Protestants who loved their King, we lit huge bonfires and feasted well.

I had already planted the wheat seed that would produce its crop next summer, when Jeremy Stickles appeared in my life once again.

On Judge Jeffreys' orders, he had brought soldiers from London to seek out any rebels. He made his headquarters at Plover's Barrows and always went to bed with a loaded musket and sword close at hand.

Jeremy told me about his mission. "There are some people who plot and others who are plotted against," he whispered. "But the cleverest are those who unravel plots. That's why I'm here. That's why Judge Jeffreys has given the job to me."

I smiled. Jeremy could be a terrible boaster at times.

He continued with his story, explaining how the Duke of Monmouth, the son of the last King Charles, had been banished from the land many years ago. Now it was said that the Duke

Jeremy brings soldiers from London

was about to land with troops on the coast of England. He wanted the kingdom for himself.

It was clear that Jeremy's job was to spy out the land and see what support the Duke might have in the area.

***

I had my own spying to do. I wanted to find out the lie of the land around the Doone Gate. If we ever attacked the valley, we would have to know what defenses the Doones had.

I traveled on a moonlit night, dodging in and out of the bushes as I made my approach.

I saw the entrance, a dark tunnel that had been cut through the cliff. A huge tree trunk hung above it. It was secured with great ropes and its purpose was clear. In times of danger, the tree could be quickly dropped to block the way.

Above the tree trunk was a gun platform from which some thirty men could have fired. I could not see any guards about, so I made straight for the tunnel.

Once inside, I came to a great oak door. To my surprise, the door was not fully closed. I looked through and saw two men sitting at a

The guards play cards in the Shadows

table, playing cards. The taller of the two addressed the other as Charlie. This must be Carver's cousin!

It seemed as though Charlie had had enough of the game and he wasn't going to play anymore. He slammed his cards down and stood up from the table.

"You keep watch. I'm going to see Lorna," he growled.

"Carver will kill you if you do," said the other.

Charlie just sneered and walked off.

I decided to follow Charlie and find out where Lorna was. He walked towards the main village and knocked on the door of a small cottage. Lorna answered, but then I saw Carver appear, rudely pushing past her.

Charlie had not expected Carver to be in the house and made the excuse that he had just come for a drink.

"No doubt you've had too much already," shouted Carver. "Be on your way!"

Carver slammed the door in Charlie's face. Charlie walked away and soon after, Carver also left. I saw him return to his own cottage. Then I crept around the back of Lorna's home and tapped on the window.

The window opened and Lorna's face appeared. For a moment, she did not recognize me. Then a huge smile crossed her lips.

"John," she whispered, "you must be mad to come here."

"There was no news of you," I whispered, "so I came to see for myself what was happening."

"The news is bad," she answered. "Sir Ensor is sick and near death. Counsellor and Carver have taken control of everything in the valley!"

I told Lorna that it was time for her to leave, but she insisted that she didn't want to think about that until Sir Ensor had died.

I said I understood and wished her good-night with a kiss, before vanishing into the darkness. I slipped back through the Doone Gate and ran home.

As I lay in bed that night, I knew that I now had a good map of the valley in my head. I knew all its secrets.

Chapter 19
Jeremy Stickles in Danger

A few days later, as I was working in a field, I heard voices. Three men, each carrying a musket on their shoulder, were walking down the hedge towards me.

They looked suspicious for they seemed to be stalking more than walking. At first I thought they were after me. Perhaps the Doones had found out that I knew the way into their fortress.

I threw myself flat on the ground and hid myself as best I could on the other side of the hedge. I hoped they would pass by. But they didn't. Instead, they stopped near me.

I looked up through the hedge and saw Carver Doone, his cousin Charlie and, the biggest surprise of all, that arrogant brat Marwood, the son of the Baron de Whichehalse.

"There's a big young fellow who lives on this farm," I heard Carver say, "and I have an account to settle with him if I ever come across

Three men with muskets

him. He's out for revenge because we shot his father."

"Oh, you mean that fool, John Ridd," said Marwood. "He's a simple farmer. He may be as strong as a bull and the local wrestling champion, but he hasn't got any brains."

"Never you mind," said Carver. "I've got a bullet ready for him. Any man who comes between me and what I want will pay with his life."

Charlie interrupted. "And we have plenty of bullets tonight for another of our enemies."

"He will be dead within the hour," said Carver, his voice creaking like a gallows chain. "Now, take your places. And don't forget, one shot at his body, two at his head. He'll be coming down that hill any time now."

I suddenly saw that it wasn't me they were after. I knew exactly who would be coming down the hill in a moment or two. It was the way he always came back to Plover's Barrows at day's end. They were waiting to shoot Jeremy Stickles.

Silently, I crawled away. Once out of sight of the three villains, I ran as fast as I could. I found Jeremy riding his horse towards the ambush. I was almost out of breath. "Jeremy! Stop!"

He was so surprised to see me that he drew his pistol and aimed it, thinking I was trying to kill him.

"No. No. Not me!" I cried. "Three men are waiting ahead to kill you. I have seen them and overheard their plans."

Jeremy did not seem surprised. "I knew someone had been watching me recently. I guessed it must be those rebel Doones. Leave them for now. They have the draw on us today."

Jeremy slapped me on the back and thanked me for saving his life. "May I do the same for you one day. You're a good man, John."

Chapter 20
Sir Ensor's Deathbed Gift

The next day I saw Tom Faggus. He galloped into the farmyard waving a piece of parchment in the air. The King had given the highwayman a pardon! For all of us who knew Tom well, that didn't give us any great hope for his future. We knew what a wild boy he could be. Just one mistake and the King would tear up the pardon.

The next day there was another visitor. Gwenny found me sitting on Spy Hill. She had been sent by none other than Sir Ensor Doone.

"The old man is close to death," she said, "and wants to see you."

"What," I cried, "does he know about me?"

"Everything," said Gwenny. "Lorna has told him all."

I followed Gwenny back to Doone Valley. I was blindfolded at the gate and then led inside, to Sir Ensor's house.

A few minutes later, Lorna and I were

shown into the old man's bedroom. I saw that Sir Ensor was not in bed, but sitting up in a chair. He was wrapped in a red cloak, his long white hair flowing down his back.

Tom Faggus is pardoned

"Do you know, John Ridd," he murmured, "that Lorna is descended from one of the most noble and aristocratic families in the land?"

"I always knew she must be of noble birth," I answered.

"And you know that you are descended from the humble Ridds?"

"Sir!" I replied angrily. "The Ridds have been honest men for twice as long as the Doones have been rogues."

The old man leaned forward. "Now listen to me, you foolish young upstart. You must promise me that you will never see Lorna again."

"I will never do that," I answered firmly.

Sir Ensor looked shocked. For forty years he had been feared and obeyed by all around him. I too was afraid of him, but with Lorna beside me I felt braver.

"So, you are not the clumsy clod, nor the country yokel I took you for," he said.

"Oh, no Grandfather," said Lorna, "nobody realizes how strong a person John is, because he is so modest."

Sir Ensor was growing tired. He knew his battle with Lorna and I was lost. We were too much in love.

"Fools you are," he said, "fools you'll be forever."

His breath was fading as he struggled to open a box on the table beside his chair. From it, he took something and placed it in Lorna's hand.

"It's my necklace," cried Lorna. "The necklace you took from me."

I looked at it closely and saw that it was a priceless item.

The next thing, Sir Ensor had passed away. It was the end of a cold, cruel life. Yet, by returning the necklace to Lorna, it was almost as if he was saying sorry for what he and his family had done to her.

I was sure now that the necklace held clues to Lorna's past.

Chapter 21
A Brave Winter Adventure

On the day of Sir Ensor's funeral, "The Great Winter' began.

An icy wind set in and snow began to fall. Within a couple of days all the fields and the hilltops had vanished under a thick white blanket.

All the creatures of the world were starving. We fed partridges and pheasants by hand. Robins and blackbirds came pecking on our door. It seemed that every creature looked to us for help.

Dear Annie built wooden cages in the barn. Many a wild creature survived the winter there, including rabbits that Betty would rather have roasted for supper.

The cows huddled for warmth in the cow-shed. We looked for our sheep but it seemed that the whole flock had vanished. Our sheep-dog, Watch, found them buried deep under the snow.

Master Fry and some laborers from nearby farms started digging the poor creatures out. One by one, we rescued them.

I carried more than sixty sheep home, two at a time, one under each arm. Hundreds more that we could not reach died on the hills.

The snow continued to fall and soon, it lay higher than our windows. We lived with the oil lamps burning all day.

One morning, Lizzie came to talk to me. Annie and I used to call her "My Lady" because of her uppity airs and graces. If Annie was meant to love and cook, and I was born to farm and wrestle, then Lizzie was made to read books. And that morning her love of reading came to my rescue.

She told me that she had been reading a book about how people lived in lands where it snowed for much of the year. The depth of the snow never kept them indoors. They walked around the country on snowshoes. We all knew what snow sleighs were because we used them on the farm in winter. But we had never seen snowshoes.

That day, I made myself a pair of snow-shoes, each having a wooden frame covered with cow skin. And after a little practice, I

Rescuing the sheep

found I could use them quite well.

I was desperately worried about Lorna, so I decided to use my new snowshoes to pay her a visit. Late that afternoon, with plenty of food in my bag, I put on my shoes and traveled to the waterfall. It had become a sheet of ice.

Tying my snowshoes around my neck, I crawled up the ice with great difficulty. Soon I was in the valley and crossing the snow in my new shoes.

I reached Lorna's cottage and hesitantly tapped on a window.

"Who's there?" Lorna called out, nervously.

Lorna and Gwenny couldn't believe I had come. They were so happy to see me, not least because they were both starving.

As they ate the food I had brought, I asked why they had not been fed.

"They won't give us any food until I agree to marry Carver," answered Lorna.

I begged Lorna and Gwenny to come to Plover's Barrows right away.

"But how can we?" asked Lorna. "The snow is too deep."

"I know a way," I replied. "Pack a few things and be ready in four hours."

Lorna and Gwenny promised they would be ready.

"Be careful," said Lorna. "And don't forget that tonight is the night when Carver Doone becomes leader in place of Sir Ensor."

As I hurried home to collect the things I would need, I thought that it would be to my advantage if the Doones were busy celebrating.

Chapter 22
Rescue

When I got back into the valley, I saw that the Doones had removed the Dunkery Beacon from Exmoor and brought it back to Doone Valley. Now it burst into flames as the celebrations began. Just about everyone living in the valley was gathered around it.

When I reached Lorna's cottage, I saw all was not well. I could hear men's voices inside. It was Charlie and Marwood. I could also hear Lorna crying.

I took off my snowshoes and charged at the door, breaking it down. Lorna was cowering in a corner with Marwood and Charlie, roaring drunk, standing over her. Blinded by fury, I grabbed both men and threw them out. Cursing loudly, they ran off into the night.

Lorna and Gwenny were very surprised to see that I had brought the farm snow sleigh with me.

"Get on, quickly!" I shouted.

John breaks down the door

The two girls grabbed their belongings and jumped on board. I hurriedly put on my snowshoes again and threw the sleigh harness over my shoulders. I leaned forward and began to pull. For a moment, I could not shift the sleigh an inch, but gradually it started to move. Once it was going, there was no problem in keeping a good speed over the snow.

We slid silently, and unseen, past the celebrations going on around the beacon. I saw Carver and smiled at the thought of the shock he would receive later that night.

We reached Lorna's bower safely and prepared for the next stage of the rescue. I had looped ropes from the top of the rocky shaft to bring the sleigh down, and now I was going to use them to get all of us up to the waterfall.

Lorna didn't pause, although Gwenny needed help to cling to the rope as she climbed. Once they had reached the top, I climbed too, then hauled up the sleigh behind me.

With more ropes fixed to rocks, we slipped and slid all the way down to the bottom. There we took to the sleigh again. I covered Lorna and Gwenny with a thick blanket, to keep them warm.

Soon we were home and Mother was the

first to greet us. She looked at the sleigh, but could only see the shapes of Lorna and Gwenny hidden beneath the blanket. Both the girls were fast asleep, exhausted from cold, hunger and fear.

I lifted them up, put one over each shoulder and took them inside. My mother put them to bed straight away.

Later, I visited Lorna. I found her tucked in bed, propped up with pillows. She was so happy to be with us at the farm, yet she knew that this was just the beginning.

"How long before Carver and the Doones come to recapture me?" she asked.

"I'm here to protect you forever," I answered, hoping that she didn't see the worry in my eyes.

Chapter 23
The Necklace

I knew that the Doones would very soon discover where their Queen was. No doubt I had been seen by Marwood. He knew perfectly well who had thrown him out of the door. He would have told Carver.

Lorna grew well and healthy in those first few days at Plover's Barrows. She was like a newly burning flame. And as her happiness warmed, so did the weather.

The wind stopped moaning. The snow began to melt and the skies turned blue. Spring arrived and with it came the first primroses. Lorna and I were so happy. Mother treated her like another daughter.

There was happy news from Tom Faggus too. He had bought three hundred acres of land to farm. So now, instead of Highwayman Faggus, he could rightly be called Squire Faggus. My mother finally agreed to him marrying Annie.

Lorna was pleased to meet Tom, and Squire

Faggus was very taken by Lorna, especially when he saw her necklace and the thumb ring she had given me. He asked if I knew anything about the pieces. I told him the story Lorna had told me.

"The ring is nothing," he said. "I would never have held up a coach for that. But the necklace . . . ye gods, it is worth as much as your farm and probably all the wealth of Dulverton too."

"What?" I replied, in deep shock.

"It is made of diamonds," answered Tom. "The finest diamonds I have ever set eyes on. Trust me. I would have stopped a coach with ten armed guards to get my hands on a necklace like that."

My mother interrupted. "Tom, you have won my daughter's heart and have promised to forget your previous trade and live an honest life. Yet here you are, yearning for a life of robbery again. I will not risk my daughter's life with a man such as you."

I don't think Mother really meant it, but it gave Tom something to think about.

Lorna asked him exactly how much he thought the necklace was worth.

Tom held the necklace in the palm of his hand and started to speak in hushed tones.

"There are twenty-five rose diamonds in this necklace and another twenty five large ones that could not be equaled in all London itself. How say you, Mistress Lorna, to a hundred thousand pounds?"

"You must have this jewel."

Lorna didn't blink, but did the most extra-ordinary thing. She took the necklace, walked up to my mother and laid it in her hand. "You have been so good to me," she began, "you must have this jewel. It is but a small payment for such kindness."

My mother, of course, said she couldn't take it. She knew it was perhaps the only thing Lorna owned that linked her to her mysterious past.

Chapter 24
The Battle for Plover's Barrows

Jeremy Stickles arrived a few days later. He was covered in mud from head to foot and cursing the Doones.

"Wicked fellows!" he shouted. "Three Doones, galloping after me for miles – they almost caught me up!"

He brought bad news. He'd been away to raise an army, to keep the peace in the area. "You Exmoor folk live in such a divided place," he said. "Some of you live in Devon, the rest in Somerset."

The men of Devon had said they would march to help fight the Doones when the Somerset men had taken the field. And the Somerset men said they would take the field when the Devon men had marched.

The result was that he still had no army.

What were we to do now? We were at the mercy of the Doones. Jeremy agreed that the

Doone attack would come soon, now that the snows had melted.

Laura spoke up. "They won't attack yet. The valley will be flooded by the great thaw. They will have to wait for better conditions before they attack."

Lorna was right, but that didn't stop one terrible thing happening soon after. She was in the garden looking across the flooded stream racing past our farm. Suddenly, she saw a pair of eyes peering out at her from the bushes on the other side.

It was Carver. He could not leap across the flooded stream, but he aimed his gun at her nevertheless. "I will spare you this time," he snarled, "but unless you come back tomorrow for our marriage, you shall die. John Ridd will die too. Do you hear me?"

That night the family set about preparing the house for an attack. We put shutters on the windows and pails of water all around the house, in case they tried to burn us out.

I tried to work out how strong we would be against the Doones. There was Jeremy, myself, three farm servants, the parish clerk and the magistrate. We had a few pistols and most of the men also had thick staves.

Carver threatens Lorna

For the next few days, I slept outside by the haystack, watching over the farmhouse with my musket in hand. I was beginning to feel that the Doones would never come when Gwenny suddenly ran down from the house.

"I can see 'em from my bedroom window," she said. "Ten of 'em are heading our way!"

A short time later, the Doones rode into our yard. I heard the deep voice of Carver whispering, "Two of you, go and make a bonfire of the haystack so we can see to cut their throats. Kill every man and child but remember, if any man touches Lorna, I will shoot him down. She belongs to me."

I lifted my gun and aimed it at Carver. I could have shot him dead that instant. I only had to pull the trigger.

And yet, I could not. I had never taken a human life before. I lowered my gun and picked up my wooden staff, instead.

Two men came towards me. Blinded by the torches they carried, they did not see me as they tried to set fire to the haystack.

I cracked the first man across the elbow with my staff and broke his arm. He gave a roar of pain and fell to the ground. The other man stood frozen in surprise. He didn't see my staff

John saves the haystack

as it hit, snapping his collarbone in two.

Now it was Jeremy's turn. He had lined up six of our number with guns on the other side of the house. As the rest of the Doones made ready to storm into the house, Jeremy ordered his mob to fire.

Two of the Doones fell dead instantly, while the others took cover. It was clear that they were not used to people defending themselves.

Carver knew he could not win. He signaled to his men and they galloped away.

After the attack, more soldiers were brought into the area and we felt safe for a while. So safe that we began to think of attacking Doone Valley ourselves!

Chapter 25
A Visit from Counsellor Doone

All my thoughts were now on marrying Lorna, although my mother said she was still too young. Another person who didn't want me to marry her was Counsellor Doone, the son of the late Sir Ensor Doone and the father of Carver.

One day he arrived at the farm, full of false charm and lies. Mother was talking to him when Lorna and I entered the room.

"My darling child, how wonderful you look," he said, smiling at Lorna. "Come, let me kiss you."

Lorna quickly made an excuse and turned away from him.

Counsellor ignored the insult and surprised everyone in the room with what he said next. "Good lady," he said, turning to my mother, "I give my full consent to Lorna marrying your son."

My mother was delighted to hear the words, but I suspected he might add a condition to that consent. He did.

"They make a good couple," he said, "and we will be happy to add him to the strength of our family. He can fight with us."

"Oh no, sir," cried mother, "he has always been brought up to be honest."

Counsellor thought for a moment. "Yes, that does make a difference. Honesty can be a disgrace for life among my family. But no doubt John can change."

"No, no!" said mother, with even more force. "He could not steal even an apple when he was a boy. He will be honest to his dying day."

Counsellor saw that he was losing the argument and turned on Lorna, asking her why she was not grateful that he was willing to give his consent to the marriage.

"I might be grateful," snapped Lorna, "if I thought for a moment that your consent was given because you loved me. And I know that you are still not telling me all you know about my mother."

"Curiosity about your mother is a fine thing," sneered Counsellor, "and perhaps out of kindness we haven't mentioned her background. But I will tell you something about your parents. Are you aware that your father killed John's father, and John's father killed yours?"

The words silenced everyone in the room.

"That can't be!" cried Lorna. "It's a lie!"

I knew it must be a lie too. "Even if it happened, which I do not believe for a moment," I said, "our love is too strong. Your story cannot break that love."

Counsellor's eyes flared red with anger. "How dare you doubt my word!"

The conversation ended there, but not the Ridd hospitality towards visitors. It was rude to refuse anyone a bed, for traveling at night was danger itself. So Counsellor was allowed to stay.

The next morning, after breakfast, Counsellor visited Annie in the dairy. He said he wanted her to show him how she made our clotted cream. And while she was showing him, he asked whether she had ever heard of a piece of magic, which helped make it twice as thick.

"All you have to do is pass a string of polished glass beads across the top of the cream churn," he said.

Annie could be a very innocent girl at times.

"Lorna has a necklace," she said. "I shall borrow it."

"Yes," he said, "but tell no one about this until our magic is done."

Annie collected the necklace from Lorna's room and Counsellor passed it three times over the churn.

"Now we must leave the room and the necklace," he said. "Do not return for a day. Then you will come back and find how the cream has thickened. Only then can you return the necklace to Lorna. But, remember, not a word to anyone until the day has passed."

So they left the room, but Counsellor made an excuse to go back in for a moment to see that all was well. He was only there for a second. He left the farm soon afterwards.

When Annie returned the next day the necklace was gone. Counsellor had taken it with him.

"Tell no one about this."

Chapter 26
Jeremy's Strange Tale

Jeremy Stickles had been away from the farm for some weeks, spying on people, trying to find out who supported King and country and who would fight for Monmouth and the rebels.

He returned in high excitement. "I have discovered something amazing," he said. "It happened one evening when I was riding from Dulverton to Watchet on the Somerset coast."

"Dulverton to Watchet!" I interrupted. "I'm sure I remember something about that road."

Jeremy told me to keep quiet so he could get on with his story. "I had just reached the coast," he began, "and was riding along a wild track above the cliffs. It was dusk, so I decided to stop for the night at a lonely little inn called the Forest Cat.

"I was met by an elderly woman called Benita. She said she could give me a room and a meal. We got to talking, and I asked her how she had come to live in such a lonely place."

***

This was the story that Benita told Jeremy.

Benita had been born in Italy. About fifteen years ago she had met an aristocratic Scottish family. They were traveling through Europe after a dispute over some land they had shared with another family in Scotland.

Benita went to work for the family, as maid to their two young children. The father had died in an accident, so the rest of the family and Benita sailed for England, making landfall on the Devon coast.

From there, they had set out for the town of Watchet, intending to stay with some friends. But they had to spend a night in the inn at Dulverton because their coach had broken down. They continued their journey the next day.

As their coach was nearing Watchet, they were chased by a gang of robbers on horseback. The coach driver tried to outrun the horsemen. But they were too quick. Eventually, the coach was forced off the track and onto a beach.

As the sea rushed in around the coach, the horsemen dismounted and attacked.

The children's mother tried to hide some precious jewels she had with her. She placed a

The sea rushed in around the coach

necklace around her little girl's neck hoping the men wouldn't find it.

Benita had remembered hearing her shouting out: "I know these horsemen. They are my family's ancient enemies!"

The next moment, Benita was knocked unconscious.

When she awoke, she found the horsemen gone and the mother and her son lying murdered on the beach. There was no sign of the little girl.

Benita had ended her story by telling Jeremy that the mother and her son were buried in Watchet churchyard.

***

"Was it the Doones who killed them?" I asked Jeremy.

"It could be no one else," he answered.

"And the little girl in the coach?"

"As sure as I stand here, that little girl was our own Lorna Doone," he said, solemnly.

At first, I was stunned. I could now clearly remember the day that Master Fry and I had arrived at the inn in Dulverton and how I had met the foreign maid in the yard. That must have been Benita.

I remembered how we'd passed the coach going up the hill out of Dulverton. I could see that coach again with the maid, the lady and her two children inside.

The horror of that night rushed back to me . . . the Doone gang passing us by Dunkery Beacon and the sight of the little child lying across the rider's saddle. "Oh, my poor Lorna," I whispered.

Jeremy swore me to secrecy about the story for the time being, and he wouldn't even tell me the name of Lorna's mother. He said he would have to report his discovery to the King, first.

In any case, he knew I could learn more by visiting Benita at the Forest Cat Inn. Indeed, I was a little afraid to discover that name because the more noble Lorna proved to be, the less chance I had of winning her as my wife.

I was also worried about what would happen if both Jeremy and I were killed in the coming battle for Doone Valley. Then no one would be left to tell Lorna about her true background!

Chapter 27
All Seems Lost

My worries about the attack on Doone Valley didn't lessen with the arrival of some troops from Somerset.

They had got rid of their officers on the way down and were now a ragbag army of cobblers, farmers and chaps who could mend kettles better than they could fight.

The sons of Devon marched onto Exmoor soon after. Their problem was that they would rather fight the men from Somerset. Jeremy was happy about that, as long as they fought the Doones first.

Altogether, the forces that gathered at our farm to attack the Doones numbered over a hundred, including fifteen of Jeremy's troopers.

The day dawned and the men of Devon, complete with one cannon, took up positions to attack from the cliffs on the western side of the valley. The Somerset boys, also with one cannon, were placed at the eastern side. The

Attacking the Doone gate

third group was made up of one cannon, Jeremy, his troopers and me. We would attack the Doone Gate.

From my position, I heard the Devon and Somerset men open fire from their high positions on the cliffs above the valley.

Jeremy ordered our charge on Doone Gate. Ten men on the platform above the gate opened fire and the air was filled with musket balls. We hurried forward, dragging our cannon with us.

We desperately needed to reach a position of safety under the enemy's platform before they could reload. This we did, but then the men above released the huge hanging tree trunk. It crashed to earth right onto our cannon. Two men were crushed and two of my horses were badly injured.

I loved those horses. Their injuries turned me into a madman. I charged through the gate. Jeremy and some other men followed.

I saw three men and flung the first against the wall. The other two ran off and escaped through the great oak door, slamming it shut behind them.

I looked back to see where Jeremy and the others were. It was a terrible sight. Two men had been killed outright by musket shot. Jeremy was injured. Some of the Devon and Somerset men had fought and died, others had run off.

The day was lost. It was a disaster!

***

A sense of gloom settled over our farm after the battle. I could not see how the Doones could ever be defeated.

There was also news from the King's Court in London. Before the battle, Jeremy had sent messages to London telling the court what he had discovered about Lorna Doone.

A few days later, two of the King's servants arrived at Plover's Barrows. They told Lorna that she should be ready to make a journey to London in a few days time. She was now to be under the guardianship of the King himself.

Meanwhile, Jeremy, still recovering from his injuries, released me from our secret. I went to tell my beloved Lorna all I knew. She was in the garden.

"So you are not a Doone at all," I said, after telling her Jeremy's story, "although I do not know your real name yet."

The day was lost

Tears began to pour down her face, but as she cried, she realized something. "My father . . . your father," she said, "couldn't have killed each other!"

"No," I replied, "Your father died in an accident."

She was sobbing wildly now and I held her in my arms. "Dear Lorna," I said, "what can we do now? We all know now that you are high born. A humble farmer like me cannot expect to marry you."

Lorna was very angry at what I said, and the tears stopped. "Am I to throw away every bit of happiness in my life just because my parents were of noble birth?"

"But the King is your guardian now."

Lorna wiped her eyes. "I love only you, John. I want no other man."

Then she asked me a question. "Would you give up your farm for me?"

"Yes," I replied instantly.

She looked me deep in the eyes and said, "And I would give up my life for you. I have to go to London, but eventually we will be together. Of that I am absolutely sure."

All Seems Lost

"What can we do now?"

Chapter 28
Lorna's True Identity

That same day I galloped over to the old inn near Watchet to meet Benita.

She did not remember me as the young boy she had seen at the Dulverton inn. But she was really excited to learn that I knew the whereabouts of the five-year-old girl she had been looking after on that day when the Doones attacked the coach.

"Would you still know her?" I asked.

"I think I might because she was the prettiest little girl."

"Then you shall see her tomorrow."

"How wonderful," said Benita, "I look forward to meeting Lady Lorna Dugal, the Countess of Lorne's daughter again."

Benita had finally said the words. At last, I knew Lorna's true name . . . Lady Lorna Dugal.

Benita told me how Lorna was the last surviving relative of the Lorne family. They were

Benita recognizes Lorna

of royal blood and it was this family who had argued with Sir Ensor Doone over the land they jointly shared in Scotland.

Now that Lorna was the only surviving child, she inherited that land.

It was at that moment that I at last understood why the Doones had kidnapped Lorna and kept her identity a secret, hoping she would marry Carver.

If the marriage had taken place, then Carver, as Lorna's husband, would have got his hands on the land the Doones had lost all those years ago.

What sweet revenge that would have been for Sir Ensor, if he had lived to see the day when he could return to his Scottish lands.

Back at Plover's Barrows the next day, Benita recognized the Earl's daughter instantly. "The eyes! The eyes!" she cried. "How could I not know you, dearest Lorna?"

"Oh Benita! Benita!" cried Lorna, falling on her former nurse's breast and breaking into deep sobs.

Chapter 29
Lorna Leaves for London

Lorna was still waiting to leave for London when I had to leave the farm to meet a man in a wrestling match in Dulverton. My opponent was a giant of a man, but he was a horseshoe in the hands of a blacksmith when I fought him.

I won the match, but when I returned home I knew I had lost something far more important. I couldn't find Lorna. I begged Lizzie to tell me where she was.

"Lady Lorna has gone to London," she said, screwing up her lips as if the title was too grand to speak of. "She has taken Gwenny too."

"What! Gone without saying goodbye?" I cried.

"She left a letter for you. It's in her room."

I ran to Lorna's room and found it.

"My Dear John," she wrote, "Don't blame me for leaving you without saying goodbye. The King's men suddenly decided we had to leave for London, and they would not wait. It broke my heart not to say goodbye to you. But remember one thing, there may be differences in our rank, but that won't stop me from loving you. I shall forever be your own, Lorna."

Her tears had stained the page and now mine were doing the same.

In the weeks that passed after Lorna's departure, I worked alone in the fields, dreaming of the day she might return. I wrote to her every day, but never received a reply. The post from London could take a month or more to reach the wilds of Exmoor. Daily, I waited for the first of my darling's letters. It never came. I was heartbroken. She must have found a better world in London. Now she was with her own people, she would quickly forget me.

For a while, I wondered if the Doones would attack again, but I knew that we were small fry now. The Doones had more serious issues to worry about. The King had heard of the battle and of our defeat. He would surely take action against the Doones now. They would be preparing to meet a more powerful enemy than Jeremy's ragbag army.

In the summer of 1685, we started to hear rumors of another army. It was said that Monmouth had landed on the Devon coast and

Working alone in the fields

proclaimed himself the King of England. We also heard that country boys from all over Devon and Somerset were joining his army.

The first piece of definite news about the rebels came from Annie. She rushed into the kitchen one morning. "John," she cried, "Tom has joined the rebels! Please, you must go and bring him back."

I knew my duty. If I didn't bring him back, then Judge Jeffreys would certainly hang him.

Chapter 30
An Old Friend to the Rescue

I set off to find Tom Faggus before dawn the next day. It was a long ride to the place where King's men and rebels had fought.

In a small town near the battlefield, a man told me that the rebels had been beaten. There had been a terrible battle and the King's men had massacred them. Sadly, he pointed in the direction of that night's fight.

What a terrible sight met my eyes! The dead and the dying were everywhere. I was kneeling over one poor injured lad, when I felt a nuzzle on my cheek.

It was Winnie, Tom Faggus's remarkable horse! She turned her head towards the main area of the battlefield as if telling me in which direction to go.

Winnie led me to what I thought was a corpse. But then the body moved. It was Tom! He had been shot in the side with a musket ball. He was still breathing. I cradled him in my

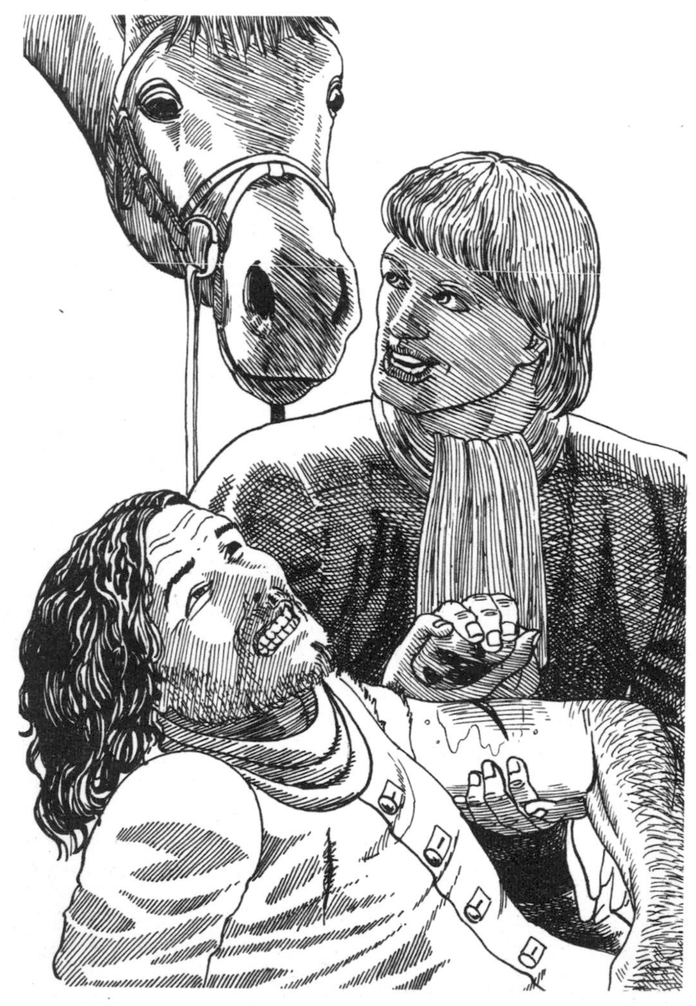

"Is Winnie alright?"

arms and tied a piece of cloth around the wound.

Between his groans, Tom only uttered three words: "Is Winnie alright?"

With great difficulty, I raised him onto Winnie's back and tied him around the horse's neck with the reins. Winnie walked off with her master. I knew she would take him home, however long it took.

I rested my own horse and later followed Winnie's path, soon finding myself in trouble. I met a troop of the King's men and they mistook me for a rebel.

"Down from your horse, rebel," they ordered.

"I am no rebel," I protested. "I am a King's man; a simple farmer."

It was then that their officer, Colonel Kirke, came over.

"Ha!" he roared. "A farmer! All the rebels say that."

In a flash, his men tied me up and dragged me to a tree. I saw that two dead men were already hanging from it. A rope was thrown around my neck. The men waited for Colonel Kirke to give the final order.

At that moment another party of men

galloped in. "Leave that man alone!" shouted a familiar voice. "He is no rebel."

The man leapt off his horse and went across to talk to the Colonel. A few minutes later, Colonel Kirke told me that he was releasing me and that I was now the prisoner of my rescuer.

The noose was taken off my neck. I was never so pleased to see my old friend, Jeremy Stickles.

"You once saved my life from the Doones," he said. "Now I have saved yours. All is equal."

He explained that I was now his prisoner, because Colonel Kirke had insisted that I face the King's Court to prove that I was no rebel.

"I have done no wrong," I protested.

"I know," said Jeremy, "but you and I must convince the King of that fact."

On reaching London, I was free to wander as long as I reported to the court each day. I spent much of my time trying to find out about Lorna.

I discovered that she was now living with an old relative, and mixing in the highest of society. The King and Queen had taken an instant liking to her.

I also found out that every Sunday she attended church at Westminster Abbey. There

John is mistaken for a rebel

was a space outside the abbey where common folk could see the Royal Family arrive. I waited there, one Sunday morning.

I saw the King and Queen enter, escorted by their most noble knights. After the knights, came the King and Queen's friends and servants. They all looked so beautiful in their fine dresses; but none so pretty as my Lorna.

She walked in with the others, her eyes to the ground. Her dress was of the purest white silk. My heart was breaking with love for her. Would she look up and see me?

To my joy, Lorna raised her eyes and turned. Our eyes met. Yet, all she did was make a little curtsey. Then she was gone. I felt I had lost her forever. I was heartbroken.

I was still waiting outside when a servant boy ran out of the abbey and placed a small piece of paper in my hand. It was a note from Lorna.

Chapter 31
The Mystery of the Letters Solved

The note from Lorna was brief. "Come and see me at noon tomorrow. All my love, Lorna." The address she gave was that of her relative.

He lived in the village of Kensington in London. I dared not go to the front door of his house, but knocked on the entrance used by the servants. To my surprise, Lorna's maid, Gwenny, opened the door. She wasn't very friendly at all. Without speaking, she showed me into a waiting room where I was left alone.

At last Lorna appeared.

"Master John Ridd," she said, with a frown on her face. "Tell me the truth. I have been in London for a long time and yet you seem to have forgotten me. Why? You said you loved me once."

"Because," I answered, "you forgot me as soon as you came to London."

"What?" said Lorna. "I sent you letters every

day, but you never replied."

"I too sent you letters every day, but you never answered me."

Lorna sighed and hugged me, saying rather mysteriously: "I think I know who's to blame here . . . Gwenny!"

There was an icy chill in the air as she called in her maid. Gwenny came in with her head hanging low, hiding her look of shame.

"Bring me the letters I gave you to send to John," said Lorna.

"How can I fetch them? I sent them," protested Gwenny.

"Gwenny!" Lorna was not to be lied to. "Bring the letters."

Gwenny's head hung even lower as she left the room. She returned a few minutes later, holding a number of letters bound with a red ribbon. They included all the ones I had sent Lorna and all those that Lorna had written to me.

"Why did you not send them?" she asked.

"Master John is just a farmer's boy," said Gwenny, bursting into tears. "You are the daughter of a Countess and descended from the Kings of Lorne. I thought you must marry a Lord at least. So I kept the letters. I am sorry."

"You'll have to go before Judge Jeffreys for this," Lorna said to the frightened girl. "Now, leave us."

I knew she did not mean to send her to the Judge. Lorna was a very forgiving woman. She proved it by her next words. "John, if you mean to marry me, then you know we will have to take Gwenny with us."

"I would take you with fifty Gwennys," I answered. "I know she doesn't really hate me."

Lorna smiled and then gave me a lecture. "Nothing can stand between us. My ancestors are not one bit better than yours, John. So do you promise to end this silly business of thinking you are beneath me?"

I did. At last I could see she truly loved me for who and what I was.

Chapter 32
Courage is Rewarded

Some very good fortune came my way in London. One night, I was leaving the house of Lorna's relative when I spotted three thieving rogues with loaded pistols breaking in. I followed them back into the house and attacked them.

I laid out the first with my staff and sent the other two tumbling downstairs. Before they could recover I tore down a curtain and rolled them up inside it. No sooner had I done that than there was an explosion. Smoke billowed from the curtain. When I unwrapped it, I found both men dead. In a panic, they had shot each other.

My luck was that these rogues were all wanted men. They were rebels and great enemies of the King. So when the King heard of my good deeds, he asked to see me.

"We are proud of you," he said. "You have proved yourself a noble and loyal servant."

Capturing some thieves

The Queen spoke too. “Our beloved Lorna has told us a lot about you.”

The King smiled and said he had a gift for me and picked up a sword. I thought for a moment he was going to chop my head off. Instead he asked me to kneel down and then he touched both my shoulders with the sword.

“I knight you, our good servant Sir John Ridd, ” said the King. “Now, arise Sir John.”

I was very surprised at this high honor. I was even more delighted when the shield bearing my new Coat of Arms arrived. There was a cow and a horse above a picture of King Alfred who, I believe, had first given Plover’s Barrows to our family. There were also some Plover birds and a field of wheat. Beneath it all was my new motto: “Ridd, never be ridden.”

My knighthood saved me from appearing before Judge Jeffreys on the charge of being a rebel. The Judge had been busy in Devon and Somerset hanging as many Monmouth rebels as he could find. When he returned, he declared me a free man.

Now I was keen to return home. My mother had been worried ever since she heard I was under arrest. I also wanted to show her my Coat of Arms to convince her that I truly was Sir John Ridd now.

Courage is Rewarded

"I knight you Sir John Ridd."

Lorna had business in London to attend to before she could join me. So I set off home alone.

Chapter 33
John meets Carver

What a journey home I had. Tom Faggus, now recovered from his wounds, had heard my news first and he had spread the word. As soon as I arrived on Exmoor, people came out from their homes to see the new knight.

And when I got home, all the family and the farm workers were waiting for me by the gate. Mother could not stop kissing me. Annie hugged me to death. Even Lizzie kissed me.

No sooner was I back in the arms of my family, than I heard that the Doones, far from keeping to their valley and out of trouble, had been back on the warpath. They were up to their old tricks again.

They had killed a young boy while kidnapping two girls from our village inn.

I went to the inn where I learned that with my new title came new responsibilities. They all wanted Sir John Ridd to go and see the Doones. I could not refuse them. So armed with a white flag to show I came in peace and a

John arrives home

bible fastened across my heart to stop any bullet should they try to shoot me, I set off for the Doone Gate. It was said that a good thick bible would stop a two-inch bullet with three ounces of gunpowder behind it.

The guards had seen me coming and Carver was waiting at the gate. "What do you want?" he said, as if he had never seen me before.

"You vile devil!" I roared back. "You know well why I am here. I am here to seek the return of our two women and to arrest the man who killed the boy."

"That's fine talk from you," he snarled back. "You stole our Queen and killed our men. Now, fool, you shall pay for it all."

With that, he leapt aside and shouted, "Fire!"

Three men sprang out from behind the great door inside the Doone Gate. They raised their muskets and fired. Fortunately, I had expected something like this and by the time the musket shot fizzed towards me, I had already dived to the floor. I wasn't going to trust my life to one bible. And before they could load their guns again, I was up and gone.

I stopped at the top of the hill and shouted back at that black-hearted villain. "Nothing will save you now, Carver Doone!"

Carver tells John he shall "pay for it all"

Chapter 34
Battle Plans

Later that day, I called a meeting at the inn. I wanted to plan a new attack on Doone Valley. The place was packed. Tom Faggus was there, and so was Uncle Ben Huckaback.

Master Fry had brought all the farm laborers with him. Most of them now had muskets and pikes. Some of the soldiers who were still in the area turned up, too.

This time we were not going to fail. We planned to finally remove the Doones from their valley. It was to happen on the following Friday night.

That evening one of our men went to the Doone Gate. He told the guards that he could tell them where Uncle Ben stored his gold.

The trick worked. Most of the greedy Doones, including Carver, rode out and followed the man to a lonely spot a few miles away. We had several men waiting for them there, and a fierce gunfight began.

A meeting at the inn

Meanwhile, the rest of us had been waiting at the bottom end of Doone Valley, ready to enter by my secret entrance at Lorna's bower. As soon as we heard the gunfire in the distance, we climbed up the waterfall, down the shaft and into the valley.

We started the next part of our plan at the first cottage. Everyone was ordered out, and then we set fire to the building. We did not treat these Doones unkindly for they were mainly women, old men and children.

We did the same to every cottage in the valley, but we made sure that no one was hurt. We even rescued the two girls who had been recently kidnapped.

The gunfight outside the valley had gone our way. We had lost two men, but those Doones who had been fooled into leaving the valley had already lost seven or eight men. The survivors then saw flames rising from their valley.

"We've been tricked!" shouted Carver. "Back to the valley, men!"

By this time, we had overpowered the last guards at the Doone Gate. We had taken up positions on the platform above the gate, our muskets ready.

Carver and his surviving men galloped

straight towards us and were met by a storm of musket fire. One Doone after another fell from their horses.

The remaining Doones fought on as best they could. By dawn, they were defeated. I walked among the dead and found that the body of Carver Doone was not there.

I did find one Doone, though. The old man, Counsellor Doone, was hiding in the bushes, trying to escape. I grabbed him and pulled him to his feet.

"Now, Counsellor, I want the truth," I shouted. "You said that my father killed Lorna's father and her father killed mine. That was a lie, wasn't it?"

"Yes," he moaned.

"Who did kill my father then? Who fired that shot from behind the haystack?"

Counsellor cowered and whispered the name. "It was Carver. My son killed your father."

Counsellor was still shaking in his boots when I asked a second question. "Where is Lorna's necklace which you stole after tricking my sister?"

"Carver has it now," he answered.

"Ha!" I laughed. "That's your last lie, Counsellor."

The Doones are defeated

I plunged my hand into his jacket pocket. I found the necklace.

I left Counsellor there and then, and to this day I have no idea what became of him.

We drank merrily in Plover's Barrows that night. It was time to celebrate.

Yet, I was not to know then that a ghostly giant of a man had been seen in Doone Valley, wandering through his burnt-out kingdom and cursing my name.

Chapter 35
Our Wedding Day

When the coach carrying Lorna back to Plover's Barrows pulled into the farm, I ran out and threw my hat into the air in excitement.

Lorna jumped out of the coach even before the horses had stopped, ran over and kissed me. I had never seen her so happy to be home. And this was her home now.

There were hugs and kisses for Mother and Annie. Even Lizzie was delighted to see Lorna back.

For a moment, she stood and looked at the beauty of the country around her. "How I love this place," she said, tears in her eyes. "The moors, the trees, the cattle, the pigs, chickens and sheep, and the wild primroses beneath the hedges in spring. Whatever my birth, I am sure I was meant to be a farmer's wife!"

***

A few days later, we went to our beautiful village church to be married by Parson Bowden. The church was filled with family and friends. People from both Somerset and Devon had walked as far as thirty miles to share our day with us.

I came to the altar first and Lorna did not keep me waiting. She came down the aisle with Annie and Lizzie behind her as bridesmaids. Every eye in the church followed her to my side.

Lorna looked like beauty itself in a pure white dress. She took my left hand in her right and smiled nervously.

Parson Bowden started the ceremony and we declared our love for each other. I was almost too nervous to look at her until she answered the parson's most important question.

"Lady Lorna Dugal," he said, "Will you marry Sir John Ridd?"

"I will," said Lorna in almost a whisper.

At last, we were married. We kissed and stared into each other's eyes with such love, a love that had begun so many years ago when we first met as children by the stream in Doone Valley. Our happiness was complete.

The roar of the single gunshot shattered the beauty of that moment. It echoed around every

Lorna is shot

corner of the church.

I stared in horror and disbelief as Lorna fell across me. Blood spread out from a single hole in her white dress. Her mouth moved as if she was trying to tell me something, some last message. But no sound came from her lips. Her eyes closed and her body went limp.

My Lorna had surely left me. Dazed with grief, I gently lowered her body to the floor and looked to the back of the church.

Chapter 36
Revenge

I knew who had done this monstrous deed. There was only one man on earth who would do such a cruel and terrible thing. I saw Carver Doone standing at the church door. He was carrying a smoking musket and ran out, before anyone could move.

I ran down the aisle and went after him. Outside, I saw he was already on his horse and galloping away up the hill. I leapt on my horse and gave chase. "Carver Doone," I roared, "it's your life or mine now! We cannot live on this earth together."

I doubt he heard my words. He dodged this way and that, galloping up mountain ridges.

My horse was the faster of the two and I slowly caught him up. He made one last effort to escape by turning towards a dark ravine.

I knew this place. I also knew that sunlight had never reached its floor. Yet, Carver knew it not. It was a dead end.

This nightmarish place was known as the Wizard's Bog. Here, at the very end, was a bottomless pit of black mud.

"It's your life or mine now!"

Carver soon knew he was in trouble. He turned in his saddle and fired his pistol. I felt the bullet hit me, and I rocked back in my saddle. But I galloped on after him, grim and determined.

Carver suddenly saw what lay ahead. With a cry of horror, he desperately pulled on his reins. His horse slid to a sudden stop.

Carver's feet left the stirrups and he was thrown high into the air. Then he landed with a thud, at the very edge of the bog.

I pulled up on my horse and leapt off. Carver got to his feet. At last, we faced each other.

"I'll see you in hell, John Ridd!" he roared, charging at me like a crazed bull. He threw his great arms around me and gripped me with the power of an iron vice.

I felt a rib snap but that only angered me more. I broke his grip and took him by the throat.

Carver tore at my hair and threw punches in every direction. Most of them missed me because he had no room to move and my grip was slowly strangling him.

There was only one way he could escape my grip and launch a new attack. And that was to step backwards. Carver made the fatal move.

With an awful cry, he slipped, tumbling backwards and into the bog.

He landed on his back, his arms flailing madly as he started to sink.

Carver and John face each other

What came over me then, I will never understand. This monster had killed my father and shot my beloved Lorna. Yet, I could not bring myself to let him die like that.

I turned and grabbed my staff and held it out to him. Either he would not, or could not, reach it. He continued to sink.

"Take hold of it," I shouted. "Save yourself!"

The sucking bog now had him by the feet, pulling him down all the time. I could no longer reach him. A ghastly glare filled his eyes as he raised his arms towards the sky.

He uttered one final curse. "Let them know in Hell that I am coming!"

Then he was gone. The last I saw of him was his fingers slipping away. The bog closed over him forever.

Chapter 37
Love Wins Out

I arrived home exhausted and bleeding from the bullet wound.

"Carver is dead," I said to my mother. "Now let me see my Lorna. I know she is dead, but I must take her in my arms one last time."

"You can't see her yet," said Mother, gently.

"Why not?" I asked. "I will see her once more and then I shall die too."

"No," replied Mother. "Annie is with her. Lorna is still alive. But she will need all her strength to survive. Lorna must be left alone."

I was left to my prayers while Annie and Lizzie cared for both of us. For days, Lorna lay close to death. It was feared that my bullet wound would end my days too.

Outside, the summer sun heated the land. The fields filled with the ripening wheat and barley. The roses bloomed and the cherries on the kitchen wall turned deep red. The waters in the stream warmed and the first brood of

John kisses his bride

larks flew happily above the hay meadows as our calves, piglets and lambs played in the fields.

Then, one sun-blessed morning, I was woken by a knock on my bedroom door. It was Annie. "Are you ready for a visitor this morning?" she asked.

The next moment Lorna entered my room. She had made a miraculous recovery. I felt my life blood return. What joy to kiss my bride again. I promised then that I would never let her out of my sight again.

Chapter 38
Story's End

And now this story is almost ended. I have little more to tell, except that, as we all knew he would, Tom Faggus slipped back into his highwayman's ways. Fighting for the rebels had put him on the wrong side of the law and the King's men were after him again.

Folk often told me that he had been caught and hanged at Taunton jail. We always knew better. With the help of his good wife, Annie, and his clever horse, Winnie, he kept the law at a distance. In later years, he did ask for another pardon. And he got it, thanks to my good friend, Jeremy Stickles.

Annie and Tom lived a loving and law-abiding life after that and had many happy children.

And what of Lizzie? She eventually married one of Jeremy's soldiers. They spent the rest of their lives reading books together. Lizzie and I did come to like each other in the end. She had, after all, been responsible for Lorna's rescue, after showing me how to make a pair of snow-shoes.

Uncle Ben grew wealthier. Jeremy Stickles spent the rest of his life eating too much and boasting of the dangerous duties that he carried out for the King.

As for my Lorna, her beauty grew year by year, as did her love for me and mine for her. She seldom spent anything of her fortune, except to help the poor in our village. She was happiest feeding the chickens or hand-rearing the lambs.

And when she was feeling mischievous and boasted of her rich and powerful ancestors, this farmer's boy who became a knight would whisper in Lady Lorna's ear, "Weren't you once just plain Lorna Doone?'

Their love grew, year by year

The End

Anne of Green Gables

By L.M. Montgomery

The folk of Avonlea are astonished when Matthew and Marilla Cuthbert, an elderly brother and sister, decide to adopt an orphan boy to help out at Green Gables farm.

But Matthew and Marilla are even more surprised when, instead of a boy, a very strange little orphan girl with red hair and freckles turns up.

Talkative, infuriating, naughty, funny and loving, young Anne turns Matthew and Marilla's life upside down.

Loved by millions of young readers around the world, this is one of the most enchanting children's stories ever written. It tugs at the heartstrings on every page.

Black Beauty

By Anna Sewell

Born on a sunlit meadow in an English village, Black Beauty has a happy upbringing and a wonderful home, with a kind and caring master.

Then the beautiful young horse is sold and separated from his friends.

So begins an extraordinary journey through life for Black Beauty; a journey that brings moments of triumph and joy, as well as pain, suffering, loneliness and cruelty at the hands of others.

Can Black Beauty ever find true happiness again? Will he find his way back to the peaceful meadows of his youth? Or is he condemned to live in misery for the rest of his life, like so many working horses of his time.

Black Beauty is one of the most moving animal stories ever told.

The Secret Garden

By Frances Hodgson Burnett

Mary Lennox is an ill-tempered and spoilt little girl.

When both her parents die, she is sent to live with her sad uncle in a rambling old manor house.

At first, Mary hates the manor house. But in the grounds she discovers a mysterious garden that has been locked up for ten years.

Even more mysteriously, she meets Colin, a sickly boy who has been hidden from the world since the garden was locked.

Mary and Colin, and their friend Dickon—an amazing boy who can charm wild animals—help the secret garden to come alive again.

And as the garden blooms once more, its special magic brings happiness to everyone in the unhappy old house.

The Wizard of Oz

By L. F. Baum

The Wizard of Oz is the famous children's story that became one of the most popular movies ever made.

Farm girl Dorothy and her dog Toto are magically carried away from their Kansas home to the mysterious Land of Oz.

As millions of children around the world know, Dorothy must follow the yellow brick road if she is ever to get home again. On her journey she meets the Scarecrow who wants a brain, the Tin Man who wants a heart, the Cowardly Lion who wants some courage and of course, the very mysterious Wizard of Oz.

This enchanting story delights at every step along the yellow brick road.